Advance Praise for
This Tenuous Atmosphere

"Told in a deeply compelling voice, *This Tenuous Atmosphere* propels the reader into a spatiality that embraces both belongingness and unbelonging. Throughout the book, Maria S. Picone etches an acute sadness originating from separation from mother and family, and a profound longing to reunite. The conflict between home and an unfamiliar place among 'ghost men' and a culture of 'destructive capitalism' drives this powerful narrative. Replete with symbolism and metaphor, the linked stories attempt to build a bridge between otherness and identity-construct. Picone's use of lyrical prose, innovative poetic forms and Korean language lends a complexity that enhances the reading experience." —**Mandira Pattnaik, author of** *Where We Set Our Easel*

"The brilliance and beauty throughout *This Tenuous Atmosphere* shines from one story to another, a fresh format awaiting at every page. Maria Picone's mastery of boundless imagination, strange yet fulfilling, makes this chapbook an unforgettable read. Be it the escape velocity or orbiting the home with a longing to return, this fine work captures the essence of immigrant life in utmost precision. Picone's words glitter and pulse with originality, so sure of their strength, I found myself captivated. *This Tenuous Atmosphere* is a true joy and force not to be missed." —**Tara Isabel Zambrano, author of *Death, Desire, and Other Destinations***

"Ghosts drift throughout this chapbook at a haunting, nostalgic, and cyclic beat. Each piece is a poetic dance. A kind of astrophysical orbit far from reach, and yet also grounded in concrete, gut-puncturing moments. You travel from Seoul subways to night skies to lunar landings, each location encapsulating different sides of one emotional truth. It feels as though gravity pulls you through the collection of pieces—narratives of home and family and heritage, some staggered and some propulsive—until you've found your conclusive whole." —**Lucy Zhang, author of *Hollowed***

"In *This Tenuous Atmosphere*, Maria Picone has created a powerful, poetic fable of being other, of the unspoken *why don't you look like us*, of capitalism and bureaucracy, of longing for place and family. With her singular voice, Picone invites the reader to worlds both known and unknown, and takes us somewhere that might be *home*." —**Cathy Ulrich, author of *Small Burning Things***

"Told in the voice of a spaceship abandoned by its mother, *This Tenuous Atmosphere* is a tale of longing for home and family, of otherness and fitting in, of assuming new and forced identities, of being confined to check boxes, then fleeing to find one's roots, and upon finding them, starting once again in pursuit of individuality and purpose. Although set in the cosmos of stars and exoplanets, light years or light seconds away, the story attaches itself close to the heart, a place of yearning to own and belong. And, that, to me, is the magic and skill of Picone's narration—her precise and poetic language, her original and hard-hitting metaphors, and her seamless integration of the real with the surreal. This chapbook is unforgettable and inimitable; it leaves a multi-blended and distinct flavor like kimchi on your tongue." —**Sara Siddiqui Chansarkar, author of *Skin Over Milk***

This Tenuous Atmosphere

This Tenuous Atmosphere

Maria S. Picone

수영

Conium Press

Portland, Oregon

This Tenuous Atmosphere
by Maria S. Picone

Published in the United States of America
Conium Press
http://www.coniumreview.com
Member of the Independent Book Publishers Association (IBPA)

ISBN 978-1-942387-21-3

Cover Artwork: Molibdenis Studio, licensed via Shutterstock
Book Editing, Design, and Layout: James R. Gapinski

This is for all the family I have or could ever belong to in the world, for all the Koreans rising from their own versions of a han story, for all who have found family in and not in blood.

Contents

Propulsion

When she knew she couldn't keep me, my mother struck a bargain with the ghost men haunting the sky. She fashioned a ship from our placenta—my fuel, her breast milk. The cost of this launch to a better life came from her ignorance, her worship of the bone-pale deities that called themselves, stars.

I achieved escape velocity. I saw the ghost men's bones for what they were: burned-up hulls. I begged to return. They said, you orbit the gravitational field of a far greater ideal. God Bless.

Arms spread, I propelled myself towards Earth. However I turned, I could never break the forces holding me back.

Exile

Every day I watched the ghost men's breath obscure the Earth in clouds of hairspray and freon.

Hometown burned within my chest, the longing to return.

Then the sun illuminated my land from space, and I glimpsed what I had lost—felt my mother's arms lifting me up, up, up.

I would not go dark.

Orbital Drift

I ran out of fuel; the ghost men gave me Coke. The first one was free, then I paid $1.99 or two for $2.99. They said how grateful they were to have saved me—how lucky I was, to have been saved.

No free rides, they said.

Moebius

The ghost men announced a war on immigrants. Pursuant to this, their government-funded craft pulled me into their gravity to check my papers. The door curled open with the surrender of a sardine tin. Apparitions in blue and white, they said nothing as they escorted me down a concrete hallway to a concrete room.

A man entered wielding a regulation pen and slapped twenty pocket flags on the table. I was familiar with these intricate symbols, although fuel cost almost three, and the copper tokens they called change weighed down my aft and fore compartments.

"We extend a warm welcome to the newest citizen of our country, the Great and Beautiful," he said, scratching at a speck of lint on his uniform. "As such, you have many rights. For each cycle, you get twenty from the government, of which five go towards hull restoration and repair."

My brain flashed to the derelict infrastructure I had passed. What restoration and repair? I opened my mouth to ask. He wrote something down on the pad. When I strained to see it, he snatched it close.

He continued, "You get a free tune up every time you circle our main station, but you have to pay a processing fee of five. Any additional repairs will be charged at normal rates."

I thought of my poor ship body, hooked up to their cold systems, starving in the grasp of Earth's invisible fist. "What about fuel?"

I didn't dare look in his eyes, but I saw his jaw contract. "You have plenty on which to survive," he said. "If you work hard, you can be anything in this galaxy."

"How do I know what to be?"

He made another mark. "I'm logging you as having paid your maintenance, your one-time citizenship fee, and your contribution to our great society." He stood and opened the door. "You are free to go," he said. The tension bled from my shoulders. With seven flags in my pocket, I did feel grateful; I could make a life here.

"Oh, but one more thing," he said as we strode down the hallway towards the docking bays. My hands shook. His eyes were blue. "Where are you from?"

Call Sign

I could never tell whether my mother gave me this name, this fragile byline no one could pronounce. Instead, they gave me a call sign that I could never tell whether it was a joke, weaponized signifier of otherness stabbed into my ears at every checkpoint: *Asia*.

Capitalism

I learned—that I needed to work, then, how, via mass transmission, scribbling down numbers and facts related to history: when the ghosts arrived, how they saved the lives and souls of the prior spirit inhabitants, how they helped the natives find their own pockets of the solar system in which to belong. This was another gratitude practice: to mark the singular way to live that was correct, I learned.

Without the ghost men's advanced knowledge, space might still be a wilderness.

As long as I could be useful, the ghost men didn't care about my background or goals. Mostly. Sometimes they asked questions prefaced with, "I'm not sure it's okay to ask this, but…" Then it always followed: "Are you really a person?" "Are you originally from here, or did you come from somewhere else?" The doubled names of Korea and Earth paralyzed my tongue, so I would just nod over and over, until their ghost eyes faded back into the spirit world and they stopped seeing me so clearly.

That was a normal job interview, I learned.

My first job was unskilled labor. Even though I was new to the system, tuning in for my daily education, I knew I had no skills. This made me feel valued, honored to be given these nebulous ghost-gifts so that I could develop competencies and gain certifications. I worked for countless cycles identifying broken-down or defunct ships, often stalled in orbit without fuel or the means to pay for it, with dead inhabitants ever becoming more and more ghostly. The flesh and bone decaying into skeletons of hulls. I hailed them over the radio and prayed for signs of life; often, nothing answered back but the static of the universe. I could see these wrecks that, like stars and systems, were constantly being ordered, retooled, decommissioned. Sometimes I recognized entities I had passed by in other cycles.

I worked hard, so the ghost men promoted me. Each day I rotated to the closest salvage flotilla, identifying pieces of wrecks they could use to construct new vessels and perpetuate the system. It slowed my Earth-orbit, but I had time off which I used to sprint ahead to the next site hub. Occasionally, I found something so valuable it was worth my entire cycle's salary, and my ghost supervisors would nod, pat me on the back, and give me half a day off.

From the scrap heaps, the junkers, the space debris of my current worksite, sometimes I would look at Earth and wonder if Mother was proud.

I wanted to turn my back on this planet

My work friends consoled me as we dismantled machines, talking in terse voices about ghostly experiences. I listened to their narratives—stories of wonder, stories of weight—and wondered if I would decommission alone. I had no loved ones in space to take me down to my components. If I had listened closely, perhaps I could have heard phantom songs of losing a home, losing a loved one in their words. But I was in pain and could not notice theirs.

In those moments, I turned to Pluto, core of rock and ice, unworthy of the notice of the ghost men. My friends taught me of the Heart, the Whale, the Brass Knuckles, observing those objects through lenses that reached further than my glasses. I plotted: where to land, what to bring, what to discover.

I asked them how far they had been. Not far, they said. We stay the course. One eye flickered leftward. The Red Planet, the ghost men were always trying to get there. Cycle after cycle our great and beautiful country expanded—easier to create new pathways than to rehabilitate old ones. Ever pushing back the native inhabitants who were trying their best to forge into new and unwrecked space where the ghost men said they now belonged. Some had relatives on the fringes who were talking about settling down, finding a new home. Some who didn't believe the ghost men anymore were talking about earning enough fuel to push out to Jupiter, maybe Neptune.

But for me, Pluto was the answer. Too far from their ambition or its destructive wake. I had become so tired of seeing the ghost men redefine their country, of reporting to work each day to vacuum up civilization, of drifting around a goal without a straight trajectory.

My friends asked me why Pluto. Pluto a paean, Pluto a dwarf hybrid planet-not-planet, Pluto a distant satellite of our Earthsun. I said I didn't know. But my left porthole could not keep a solid line of sight.

They could not know about the arrhythmia in my engine that threatened to turn me out of proper course. I would land inside the Heart around perihelion. I would circulate there, tidally locked, or land and wander until my alloys iced over such that my core never burned.

But to them, I could never admit it, so I summoned my shiniest plating and pretended to have forgotten the way, the wanting, of home.

Verification Check

After many cycles working as Asia—saving the wrecks of wrecks to solder to other wrecks—I had to renew my license to stay in the ghost country. It turned out my mother's bargain had not covered me when I could be self-sufficient, that I, as a terrestrial, had to recertify my existence at least once every three cycles. The government career success and evictions counsellor told me so, his sunglassed eyes exuding sympathy. This renewal purported to hurt, and cost me most of my savings, I complained.

"If you feel your income is insufficient, you have the option to enroll in our Elite Training Program, make something of yourself."

A friend of mine from a few cycles back had enlisted. "How does it work?"

"You pay two per application request," he said. "When you are matched with a suitable program, you take out a loan for two thousand. We take ten per cycle as repayment. You could earn up to one hundred per cycle if you do this."

"Up to—what's the minimum?"

The counsellor paused, and, shielding his heart with his clipboard, made a big scrawl. "Minimum income post Training School is twenty-five per cycle. That's at least a 20% increase in lifetime earnings."

I leaned forward in my chair. "Is that the only option?"

Frowning, he detached a flyer from the clipboard. Bright cheerful colors sang-shouted, WELCOME TO THE FUTURE YOU—IN SPACE! "You can read relevant information here." I looked it over, but there didn't seem to be any information, just marketing lingo and photos of grinning ghost men linking hands with terrestrial minority besties.

He pushed a black and white form at me. "If you're interested, fill this out. The deadline is tonight at midnight and you will hear back from the training program within two cycles."

I rolled my eyes but started answering. I lost myself in

the excruciating details of where I'm from, what my six-year goal is, how I think AI will change the future. It was like a job interview on paper.

I made it to page 18, voluntary demographics. It took all my strength to check the box that said *Other Asian* and sign my name as if I agreed. As I mouthed the syllables that leaked out under my pen, I closed my eyes and thought: Mother, I am making a name for myself in this new country.

What was the point of life, I wondered, but salvaging

"Making progress!"

Keep head down. Focus. Move to wreck. Find parts. Is this one worth three, four? Check secret places unsecreted after an overtime of revelations. These models have circuitry within what appears as walls. Is it a ripe field, an organ donation? They do not feel—do not feel for them.

Smile at coworkers but keep the steel fan over mouth so they don't see when it goes sour. *Asia.*

Ask open-ended questions to the guy who cuts your deals. He'll round up your earnings while talking fantasy football, awarding himself invisible points for his imaginary sport.

"It's time for your annual performance review."

Don't be better than the others, but be better, but appear not to be better, but appear to be better, but appear to not know that you are better.

Dread the words, *Asia's different.*

Save the aggression like the change in your spare compartments. Let it jangle until it's enough to turn into a pocket flag, green and greasy, flat and written and smoothed out.

Focus. Keep head down. Make money. Spend money. Cycle.

"You'll get that promotion next time. Just keep doing what you're doing."

Take a long time to realize that instead of making progress, your trajectory is a loop.

Stall Out

I lost track of how many cycles I had spun around my planet, a dizzying embrace turned fixation. I drank too much Coke. I tried to haul cargo and got stuck not knowing whether to move backward or forward. My application went unanswered—I never found a free time slot for the interview in the system. No one told me what to do and each time I asked for help they sent me to a different department. Around and around these bureaucratic crosspaths I circled and circled until I, sticky with fuel remnants and shaken, shaking I fell—

Crash Landing

The Emart parking lot was wide and obvious from space, a slate grey plot point for my level of urgency. Small by ghost men docking standards, I left an obvious impression in its delineated plain and scared people off their smartphones. An ajumma chastised me for getting so tan. An onlooker picked up my charred body and offered me a gift set of Spam and good Korean ginseng. The doctor saw me right away, apologizing about the shattering costs of healthcare. Treating me cost less than the price of seeing a movie in the ghost country. The pharmacy told me I had to wait twenty minutes, so I wandered around Emart browsing dinnerware and cheap toys. I stared at the rack of A- and B-cup bras and wondered where I fit in. To feel better, I bought a shirtdress in earth tones, a skincare set with ingredients from Jeju Island, a blue plastic recorder, and five boxes of 3-minute jjajang sauce.

The government set me up with a stipend, something about reparations due to inquiries from the Truth and Reconciliation Commission. They installed me in a Seoul apartment smaller than my ship. They gave me a single pot, a single plate, a single silverware set, and a wooden spoon. I stored my spare linens next to my spare noodles and my underwear in the nightstand drawer. A grinning cartoon tiger prowled the cover of my bank book. Americans might mistake it for a slim comic or an indie chapbook, but I knew better. I knew how to be a good little capitalist.

I had no skills that could be useful to this culture but the teaching of an exogenous language. I taught from 9 to 1 each day, sharing my fluency in cultural colonization with youth accustomed to erasing themselves to the ghost men could admire them. From 1 to 5 I lingered in the building, a not-Korean-not-ghost in a high tower, staring out the window at the children practicing sports in the school fields. At all times, I longed to exceed. I imagined myself getting off the bus one day after school and ascending those skyscraper apartments like a beanstalk to the stars. Pluto dimming my heart at its magnitude of 14.4. I made enough money—I learned about my birth culture—but discontent thickened in my arteries, a malaise I couldn't retail therapy away.

Call Sign II

Instead of reclaiming my name in my birth land, the government sustained use of my legal call sign: *Asia*. To them, I had been a Korean living overseas. Now I was a Korean living overseas living in Korea, and my original identity had been scorched off our family's records by the launch. I wrote this monster name in painstaking Hangul, 아시아, even though the first name itself was as long as most full Korean names. Something about the unbalanced symmetry of its syllables felt perfect to me—I had left; I had come back more encumbered than before.

Endsong Story

, once and future—an adoptee
knows the door swings in both directions—I am certain
I have lived with my mother,

> I was being certain

I will live with my mother,

> I have been certain

I was live with my mother,

> I am certain

I live with my mother,

> I will have been certain

I live with my mother,

> I have

my mother,

Reunification

I, unused to ambling the ground—I, landwalker with ship engine heart and forward thrusters—stalked through Seoul streets with gaited questions and saw her everywhere. Mother. Mothership. I saw her nowhere. On the precipice of giving up and speaking my loneliness into the sparkling lights of buildings that ambitioned the stars, I sought the refuge of the ghost men's cuisine in Itaewon. As I turned into the gated seating, her dark hair made white streaks against the sky. I gasped—it was her, it was her.

I found her.

I grasped her like all precious things should be held: desperate and tender. She called me stranger until she saw the scorch marks of launch and re-entry like tattoos on my face. Then the name that laid dormant under my call sign burst from her pruned lips like a thing jettisoned. She told me she had been waiting for me.

She told me she had not been waiting for me. That in fact waiting was more than she knew how to do, for she had not known whether I was alive. I tried to cover my burnt cheeks with something other than my own starry tears. She lifted my hair up and up. She wanted to see.

She told me waiting was a thing you do when you have hope, that she could not wait for me because she didn't have the knowing of how to wait. The information had long been fixed in orbit, neither hers nor mine to access without permission. It was the property of courts and laws and jurisdictions, like so many of the other tools used to officiate space. A concept long since become unreal.

In between my sobs, I noticed I had docked in the gravity field denoted by her heart. I could not have pulled away with all the Coke or rocket fuel in the world.

She asked me for everything. How can you compress a life into these little garbled transmissions? I did what I could. There were many instances where the line held strong, but perhaps the meaning was more than I could explain in my broken language, with my ungainly hands.

We did what we could. I got the impression that we had both been drifting closer together until finally locked into this tidal moment we could move together at last. There was no other experience I had been waiting for my whole life, and I could have dreamed it. I could have dreamed it, except for the certainty that I know my birth mother's hug.

Beginningsong Story

I am   with my mother,

laughing

mourning the aphelion and perihelion of Korea

chitchatting

watching *Game of Thrones* S1-7 reruns

marking as read the text thread I have been sending

discussing the best angle to avoid Korean Air to
LAX over Incheon

looking at old photos

debating the ethics of K-pop idol military service

heading up to the restaurant now

I have   my mother,

Exhaustion

The day was normal; the Seoul subway ingested me like a parasite at rush hour and spat me out at mom's. Slumped in my seat like a half-cooked noodle, I looked no different from the others I sat among, no call sign hanging neon spectacle over my head.

There had to be more than this, I was wondering, analyzing the sexy cell phone poster girl and her white rabbit skin. In Korea the standard of beauty was to look like a ballerina if you got the eyelid surgery. I looked to the left. A long line of black-clad crows perched on the seats pecking away at their phone screens. I swiveled my head.

A swan lake woman held the hand of a little bowl-cut boy, maybe six or seven. He was wearing a red and blue button down and grey wool coat that screamed New York twentysomething professional. He swung off the pole like a Mayday streamer. "Eonni, are you a pop star?"

No one in the vicinity seemed interested, even the woman. She held his hand like a ham sandwich. I understood—spacewalking could be perilous. The boy's eyes tried to breach my hull. "Me?"

He bobbed his head. The day pinged at my phone. For an instant I felt like I lived outside myself, like I was reading a storybook of my life narrated to a set of criss-cross applesauce students. I saw my life as he did—a great rocketing train—not as the head banging through byways with the mantra *change my life, change my life,* pulling me through. The lives superimposed one on another. I could salvage this machine for a good deal of money and take its propulsion for my own, drink it down in cool sips of Coca Cola. Instead, I shook my head back at him. I reached in my purse to grab at the treats I kept for my students. I could find that detritus by touch, much like the best parts with the finest chips and semiconductors: a toy spider ring, lychee jellies, cute animal erasers…I excavated a handful of stuff and offered it to him. "One," I advised him in that teachery tone that always felt strange from my ventilation system and intake tube.

He tugged too hard on the woman and almost fell. My fingers closed tight around plastic spider legs.

She fired Korean-language syllables at him like alphabet soup coming from a pressure hose. I could only catch a few letters here and there, mostly the crisp scolding 아s and 야s of direct address. When she turned the wings of her jacket flapped under the fake sun in the subway car. Her jet stream Korean hit me head on. Then, I was exposed; my poor vowels and blinking eyes losing me the yoke, and like a rubber band my mind reverted from 아시아 to *Asia*, the sad not-really-Korean Korean struggling to say a few words to you, kind swan creature. She meant it as kindness, the English that fell like feathers each formed and carefully plumed, but it was still better than my Korean. "Is it okay for you?"

I realized that, unlike my ghost country impulse to turn to poison and sexual subversion and coercion etc etc that she simply had been scolding him for being presumptuous and for bothering me. "Of course it is," I said, and, to assuage my feelings, added, "I'm a chodeong hagyo teacher."

Underneath her natural-looking makeup and the illumination of the bright light, a person stared out like a systems engineer. She stripped me to base components and reassembled me as a different function. In a low and too-casual tone for me to catch she spoke to him, native to native. I didn't hear but I felt it, a screwdriver twisting in my skin.

The boy approached me like you would a caged animal at the zoo. He took the spider ring with the gravity of a peace treaty and resumed looking all around. Not at me, anymore.

I watched him twisting it, twisting it ever around the same part of his finger. The arachnid danced right to left, caught by the body it encircled. As they got off at their stop, I watched him switch sides so he could take her other hand. Failure surged in as the subway picked up its pace: *change your life, change your life, changeyourlife.* My body buckled; not enough caffeine. After Nambu and SNU together, there were seats for the choosing, and I folded into one, clutching my purse to my lap as though I could hold my tears in the leather bag. Even though I had only worked my regular hours, I wanted to stick my head in the black dark space and never undock again. Inside the bag, tracing its machine-stitched threads, the desire for a different everyday surged like the living creature it had once been. It was, of course, a normal day.

Coming out at my stop, I unspun myself from the yeok and walked the gray blocks to Mom's. The steps tapped out a different tune: *do this for her*. Each one grew me a little taller, a little more hurried to see her. My breath quickened and my heartbeat wavered. The Seoul rainscape blurred a little more.

Even before I made it to the hallway to her apartment, she threw open the door, her arms. I latched on with the grace of a little child and wept.

Launch Sequence

One day after work, laying on the couch looking up at the plastic constellations on Mom's apartment ceiling, she told me about my father. This was a gift that she unwrapped like a set of ginseng.

Father: a person long forgotten, even more secret and less possible than the woman with whom I had shared one body for nine months.

He is no longer with us, she said. At first a purple and blue streak of sadness meteored across my gut, but then she explained that he had gone into space to look for me many years ago, and it had been equally long since his last transmission. I was stuck on the angles of those stars, the cheap glow of dark shapes unsticking themselves from the firmament, until she tilted my head into the cool logic of her eyes. She said, you must go and look.

No, I said.

She said, I will be here for you. I will always be here for you. She told me, as my portholes condensated, that she was the sky I could fly in, she was the land I could use to fix my path, she was the void that suspended the Earth like a necklace around the Sun. I could go and look anywhere and see what we were to each other. He is proud of you too, she added.

We tore apart like two vessels undocking, her atmosphere detaching from mine. I stabilized in what of me was myself and what was her. So much of her I had never been able to see in myself.

I left her.

It had been done once before, and I longed for it to be that way again. The leaving as a baby hurt less in the moment although it hurt all life long; the leaving as an adult hurt like a death in the span of a moment—it burned I packed it burned I launched it burned I burned

Reclamation ~ Lullaby

I could never fall fully back into old cycles, even though my supervisors welcomed me back with shit-eating grins. "How'd the training program go?" they asked. Everyone assumed I had gone there and come back, chastised, like an Icarus who flew with the educated for a brief moment but couldn't maintain trajectory. Even I could have believed it, but for the signs.

1. They sparked when I turned on the soldering iron and wove the looping pathways of old haunts, catching my attention in a secret smile to myself.
2. My mother's transmissions could only reach me from a certain point, but line by line she sang to me.
3. I was looking for someone.
4. Not a wreck.

I held this new knowledge close to my chest as I flew with outstretched arms around the Earth's little marble.

우리 아기 착한 아기

The days blew hard exhaustion in my vents. I cared less than before but I made more money; I found salvage everywhere.

Everywhere, there was something to be saved.

There—the remnants of friends who needed honoring. The hum of engines long passed into night.

소록소록 잠들라

I asked: "Have you seen another man like me?" No one thought I meant another vessel. Time pinched their faces more and more and round eyes shuttered like crescenting moons. I kept working, cycling forward.

하늘나라 아기별도

My mother'd thought they were stars, these ghost men, but the real heavens lay far from our grasp.

I poured out the conversations I'd smiled behind my metal guise and kept inward to friends, reunited—some sparkle of the truth. They leaned in to speculation, exhaust coming hot on my viewscreens.

Perhaps my father was a star.

Even more than three-quarters into my revolution, I let nothing touch me of the despair that had nearly driven me dark. I sipped Coke and thought about tomorrow. When I found the biggest haul of my career, my supervisors tried to placate me with a half-day. I polished my portholes and demanded more money instead.

엄마 품에 잠든다

Father was waiting. Just as Mother had told me she had waited and not waited. I had nothing but the love that bent spacetime: a thing more powerful than hope, that could never be salvaged because it could never be wrecked.

Tractor

I was prepared when they pulled me into orbit: my ID out, papers folded up under my arm, opening the airlock before they could impress the urgency of their core mission upon its metal threshold.

It could have been the same man who took my credentials as the last time or a new model of standard ghost man. I watched the mole on his neck not hidden by his uniform palpitate like a data hub. "I'm looking for someone."

The mole contracted as the head swiveled. "Excuse me?"

"He is a gwisin, not a regular guy."

The examiner pulled off his radiation shield sunglasses and spoke as slowly as his lips could go. "A gishing? What the hell's that?"

"GWI-SIN," I said again, slurring the S like a drunken noodle. I could almost see the sibilance enter and slide off his brain like a thwarted parasite. Sighing, I spoke the language he could understand. "He is Asian, like me."

"Oh!" His face illuminated like the sun over the Han River. "I know who you're talking about! He looks just like you!"

I closed my eyes for just a second, hoping it was actually because the man was my father and not because, to the ghost men, all exoplanets appeared the same: distant, round-faced, strange. "Please, if you could tell me where to find him." For a second, my voice quavered. The heart alarmed inside my vessel—what if he saw how much it meant? What if I, finally, saw how much it meant to me?

The examiner lowered his voice, as captivating as the tractor beam that had sucked me into this organizational body. I leaned in. "He's on the moon."

I ejected words of gratitude. The force pulling me into the ghost men's regulatory body relented. Impressed with my citizenship records, he shook my hand as I recast myself into my ship body. "It's a pleasure having you as part of our Great and Beautiful." Even though I perhaps couldn't speak the words he wanted, I could beam a smile at him, look as an equal into his eyes. Something to salvage from this wreck.

Legacy

Father did not know how to be a ship. It was Mother's heart that was vessel, always looking at how to propel itself forward. Through the poverty, through the shame, through the pain of the Korean nation birthing itself, she had always found a way. Father, I found marooned on the backside of the moon. Without oxygen, fuel, or social media, Father had become a different kind of ghost—not a ghost man but a real Korean gwisin.

Because Father couldn't escape gravity, I asked him what he wanted to do. He told me he played poker with the moon hares and tried to find the craters that tasted the most like cheese. I accused him of mixing metaphors and he just smiled. I tried to siphon him into my ship by reversing the expulsion of air as though I were vacuuming him up like a bug. It didn't take.

All the while, he clapped and laughed with praise at my resourcefulness. You are like the blind man's daughter from the story, he said. I had never heard that story so all I could imagine was the three blind mice. It was too easy to see a father mouse, a mother mouse, a daughter mouse, in the story. Cut off tails. It was getting late in the day, and I knew Mother was expecting me. But I couldn't leave him.

What if I teach you how to fly? I asked. Don't you want to go back to Earth?

He slid open the hatch of his chest cavity—there, shining and white, sat a moon rock, weighting him, unbalancing his flight. Standing up straight, holding aloft my laborious ship's fins, I tried to convey how I had become proud of my hybrid vessel. He shook his head, unwilling to try.

I got comfortable. I played the recorder I had bought in Seoul and showed him the state of my bank book. Good, he said as he passed an arm through my shoulder. I didn't know what else to do, so I spooned the three-minute jjajang mix into the bowl and heated it with the flare from my rocket. Its smell permeated the moon like a meatball slathered in marinara sauce. Good, he said as he twitched insubstantial nostrils; I would have laughed, but legacy is not comedy.

I'd missed the transit to Korea; I'd have to slingshot

myself in a figure eight around the Earth to get back. I should go, I said finally, frowning at my failure. The moon rock winked like it was mocking me. I promised to visit, and he asked me to bring him a hot bowl of hobakjuk. I couldn't imagine how I could transport it, but I agreed, of course. He had gone looking for me and ended up here. I would give him anything he wanted.

As I set up a launch pad, he passed his whole body through mine and stood there, inside and around and between and enveloping my outline. Even if father wasn't a ship, he was still part of me. Did you find your mother, he asked. Yes, I said. He jumped up and down and even though I couldn't see his eyes I could almost feel the weight of the emotions in our shared hearts. Tell her I love her, he said.

I'm on my way back to her now, I said.

He stepped outside of me—suddenly we were two distinct beings again. Don't.

What? I had already plotted my course.

My father waved his arms like a tourist taking a photo.

She told me how she gave you away, he said. You found her, and you found me. Now you go, he said, jerking his thumb out away from the sun. You go find yourself.

I shook my head again. I can't, I said, not until I know you are both secure.

Was it he who stared so, or the moon rock blinking me down? Do you not think I'm serious, I finally said, given that I now had to recalculate my angle of approach.

He showed me his palms. I do, he said. Then I'm not going to tie you here. Teach me how to come back.

Hard work, floating among barren craters, shivering on the dark side and sweating on the sun side as the impenetrable Earth rose into our field of vision. I lost count of how many cycles passed, how many times I had to refuel myself and skip back down to the yielding surface of the moon. Father's favorite recorder song was Brave by J. Lo. I was getting better too, I thought, as I practiced until music became one of my systems. And my imperfection encouraged him.

I watched Father start to roar and kick and agitate the

small patient rocks on the surface of the moon. Growing a heart with propulsion, he said, and I could feel him winking at me.

A ghost could be like a ship, I learned. A ghost needs no fuel beyond the memory of what had been.

At last, the moon stone thunked from his heart and shattered, becoming space dust. He lifted off; his engine soul shrieked into the void.

Father was fast when he had resolve. I charted our path back home, catching up to him as a sweaty and disheveled mess. Sorry, he said as I pulled alongside him. I didn't know if I could escape until I did. I smiled.

The bright band of the Earth came quickly; Father's heart sputtered and his vessel slowed.

Speed up! I called. You will crash!

I can't, I can't! he called, panicking, I reached out and touched solid mass. I wrapped my arms around him, a tandem hug, and gave him the lift to part the veil around our planet.

Reunion

We, not broken but extended into the forms in which we found a necessary living, practiced at the art of being together until we, family, became what we professed. I got my old job back. It paid more than Mom's work washing dishes in the back-end chaos of a Seoul fried chicken joint. Mom didn't want to retire. All Dad wanted to do was retire. Our rural home, far away from the noise and air pollution of the big city let me stare out at the dazzling stars that once had been my canopy, my right. Mom cooked Dad's favorite meals and left them for him to savor, silently opening his mouth wide like a cat to scent them down into the annals of his throat. Dad played poker with the moon rabbits and slept in the sun underneath the oak trees. Dad was a big hit when he came to school for Halloween. I taught my students about the ghost men's culture and language; he floated out of the wall and said Boo. Then he told jokes until the snot on their faces was half from fright and half from laughter. When he drifted through the air I heard the engine's beat keeping him aloft. The kimchi was good and the sky was clear. I bought a telescope and taught my parents how to find the planets and the major stars. Sometimes the kids asked me if I was a gyopo. Sometimes they treated me like just another learner. They never asked about vessel, I assume because they didn't wonder how to survive. The day was for working, speaking, talking talking talking, and the night was for flying, low and controlled like my desire to reclaim skies. We went on vacation to Jeju Island. Mom insisted on flying economy. Dad insisted on flying business. I just wanted to fly. As the Korean darkness fell upon us as silent as a velvet throw, I traced the stars with my finger on the window.

Lullaby ~ Reclamation

When Father cried insubstantial tears, when Mother traced the plasticity of the stars with a dull targeting UI, I knew the wreck of old Korea, our country, had crashed in their hearts and only recently been salvaged.

1. Even when I asked him, the old haunt, to go to school with me, he shrugged and said he felt too real.
2. My Korean language skills needed a lot of oiling, but line by line I sang to her.
3. We grew into each other like a smarthome system.
4. Hybridize.

I sang to my parents sleeping on the couch, covered in plaid blankets. I improvised from what I knew. I didn't know enough. I knew too much.

우리 엄마 착한 엄마

I emerged from the classroom sweating and with pinched heels. The rural air aided my ventilation system.

A pine needle, blue and perfect, blew down to my feet.
Everywhere, there was something to be saved. The hum
of gwisin long passed into night.

우리 아빠 착한 아빠

Rebel Wing

Mom caught me soaring over Hallasan in low orbit, pulling beside me with a grace I could never match. Nothing is forever, she told me.

But love.

But we, your father and I, we can keep this home fueled till you come back.

The leaving was not a leaving because there would be a return. I charted a trajectory soaring up, high above the Earth, above the ghost country that blew pollution like a ring of Saturn, into the wilds of far space.

엄마 품에 잠든다.

Call Sign III

It was enough to be, daughter, to hear, in the mechanical
thrummings of a bipedal culture,
a stilling, cosmic, once and future

소록소록 잠들라

shhh
shhh

우리 딸

Tail

I will surpass you. I will be
       brilliant. I will rise past the ghost men,
the dead hulks of history,
       our legacy of mistakes
Mother.
       I am what you projected,
the collision vector you averted, but I am also
       what I made myself: Asia, your daughter.
Father.
       I am what you protected,
the mechanism begun in utero, but I am also
       what I make myself, 아시아, 우리 딸.

When you miss me, come into our backyard, the sky
plaited with stars. Unfurl your point of view over the
length of a telescope.

There, can't you see me? Aren't you proud?

About the Author

Maria S. Picone/수영 is a queer and neurodivergent Korean American adoptee who won Cream City Review's 2020 Summer Poetry Prize and the first ever Louisa Solano Memorial Emerging Poet Award from *Salamander*. Her poetry chapbook, *Adoptee Song*, will be published by Game Over Books in 2024. She has been published in *Tahoma Literary Review*, *Vestal Review*, *Salamander*, *Orca Lit*, *Fractured Lit* and more including *Best Small Fictions 2021*. Her work has been supported by The Juniper Institute, The Watering Hole, Lighthouse Writers Workshop, GrubStreet, Kenyon Review Writers Workshop, and Tin House Writers Workshop. She is *Chestnut Review's* managing editor, *Uncharted Mag's* associate editor, and assistant fiction editor at *Foglifter*. She holds an MFA in fiction from Goddard College. Find out more at mariaspicone.com, Twitter @mspicone.

Acknowledgments

"Propulsion" was originally published in *Fractured Lit*. "Legacy" was published in *Kaleidoscoped*, and "Reunion" in *Exposition Review*. Many thanks to Tommy Dean, who not only agreed to publish "Propulsion" but whose teaching and mentoring have guided many of my flash and Alissa Tu, whose hand helped guide "Legacy" to its best form. I appreciate the lens and guidance of James R. Gapinski, and the care taken with my manuscript from beginning to end with Conium Press.

Much love to my Fig writing group, Reina and Jessica, for last minute comments, motivation, and a place to write every week, and to the Verge's Karen J and Susanna for providing support and encouragement. Linsey Krolik, Nadia Staikos, Brooke Randel, and D.E. Hardy also provided feedback and encouragement on an early draft that helped me continue this project thanks to their excitement and astute comments as part of a *Chestnut Review* asynchronous weekend workshop.

This chapbook was conceived with help from workshops and events at AAWW, Kundiman, Literary Cleveland,

Boston Writers of Color, The Speakeasy Project, VONA/
Voices, Lighthouse Writers Workshop, GrubStreet,
SFWA's Nebula Conference, Murphy Writers, and
Longleaf Review workshops. I would especially like to
thank The Juniper Institute for providing me a place
to write, and the breakthroughs made on certain parts
of this project including "Reunification," which was
written via phone dictation stumbling around the lovely
western Massachusetts campus around sunset one night
and sobbing to myself under its welcoming trees.

www.ingramcontent.com/pod-product-compliance
Lightning Source LLC
Chambersburg PA
CBHW061500210726
48287CB00007B/2600